Peeps in Pajamas

By Andrea Posner-Sanchez
Illustrated by Ron Cohee

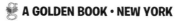 A GOLDEN BOOK • NEW YORK

What do the Peeps do at the end of the day?
They get ready for bed.

But I'm not tired.

Some Peeps wear **striped** pajamas.

Some Peeps wear plaid pajamas.

Time for all the Peeps to go to sleep.

I'm really not tired.

Maybe reading stories will help the Peeps chick get sleepy.

The Peeps pick out their favorite books
and read them together.

Some Peeps fall asleep, but the Peeps chick asks for more and more stories.

Maybe a pillow fight will help the Peeps chick get sleepy.

Pillow fights are **fun!**

Pillow fights can also be messy—and tiring.
Some Peeps fall asleep on the feathers.

Maybe a dance party will help the Peeps chick get sleepy.

The Peeps **hop** and **bop** to the music.

Before long, the Peeps chick is the last one dancing. All the other Peeps have fallen asleep.

The Peeps chick climbs into bed . . .

. . . and falls asleep. Sleep well, Peeps!